This Little Tiger book belongs to:

_____

_____

_____

For Roan, with love ~ R G

LITTLE TIGER PRESS LTD,
an imprint of the Little Tiger Group
1 Coda Studios, 189 Munster Road, London SW6 6AW
Imported into the EEA by Penguin Random House Ireland,
Morrison Chambers, 32 Nassau Street, Dublin D02 YH68
www.littletiger.co.uk

First published in Great Britain 2007
This edition published 2016

Text and illustrations copyright © Ruth Galloway 2007
Ruth Galloway has asserted her right to be identified as the author
and illustrator of this work under the Copyright,
Designs and Patents Act, 1988

A CIP catalogue record for this book is available from the British Library

Printed in China • LTP/2700/4273/0222
10 9

Tickly Octopus

Ruth Galloway

LiTTLE TiGER
LONDON

Down in the ocean, among the swirling
seaweed and the colourful coral,
lived a tickly octopus.

He had eight twisty, twirly tentacles
and he loved to use them to tickle.

When Octopus tickled the little fish
they jumped and jiggled and wriggled and giggled!
They thought tickling was wonderful fun!

But most of the creatures found his tickling tiresome.

Octopus tickled Starfish and made her squirm! "Stop it," she squeaked.

Octopus tickled the clickety-clackety crab and he tripped and tumbled into the sand. "Go away!" he snapped.

"But I'm a tickly octopus, and I'm really good at tickling," said Octopus sadly, and he swam off to tickle the wriggly, giggly fish again.

One day Octopus saw Oyster snoozing among the seashells. He couldn't resist giving her just a teeny tiny tickle.

But Oyster woke with
a jump and dropped her precious pearl.
PING! BIP! BOING! It bounced over
the rocks and was swept away by the current.
"Oh no!" gasped Octopus.
Poor Oyster was very upset.
"Sorry!" said Octopus. "I'll get it back for you."

Octopus raced through the water
with a WHOOSH! and a SWOOSH!
"Whee!" he thought. "I never knew I could
be so super speedy!"

Octopus followed the pearl as it tumbled down to the bottom of the sea. "Wow!" he thought. "I never knew I could swim so deep!"

At last Octopus reached
the pearl but . . .
PLINK!
PLONK!
PLOP!

Oyster's precious pearl bounced
over the rocks and dropped
down through a tiny gap in
the ocean floor.

Octopus squished and squashed
and heaved and squeezed . . .

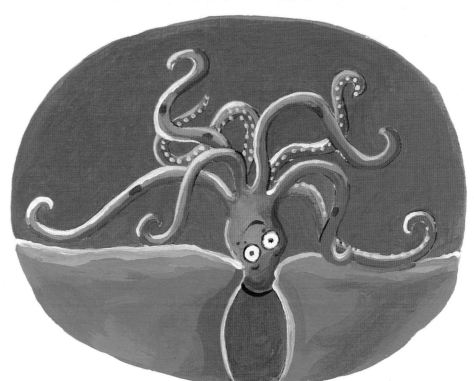

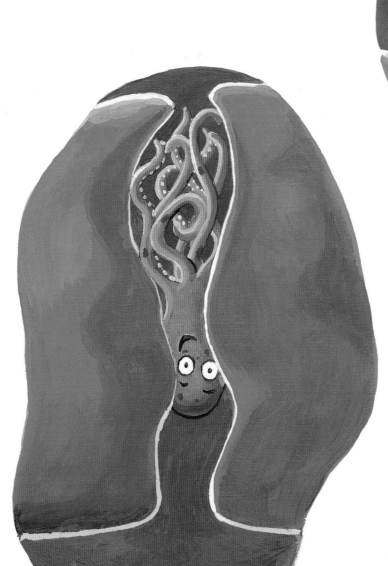

and managed to push his
rubbery body through the gap.

"Ooh!" he thought. "I never knew
I could be so squidgy!"

There, glinting in the darkness, was the smooth and shiny pearl. But just behind it was a fierce eel.

"Aaargh!" squeaked Octopus.
He quickly picked up the pearl
and sped away.

Octopus huffed and puffed as the eel chased after him.

He'd swum such a long way and he was very tired.

The eel was getting closer and closer . . .

With a spurt and a squirt, a belch and a squelch, Octopus sprayed a cloud of black ink so that the eel couldn't see a thing!

"Wow!" thought Octopus.
"I never knew I could be so inky."
And he danced happily back to Oyster.

Oyster was delighted to get her pearl back.

"I promise I won't ever tickle you again," Octopus said.

"I've found lots of other things I'm good at doing too.

From now on I'm going to be a . . .

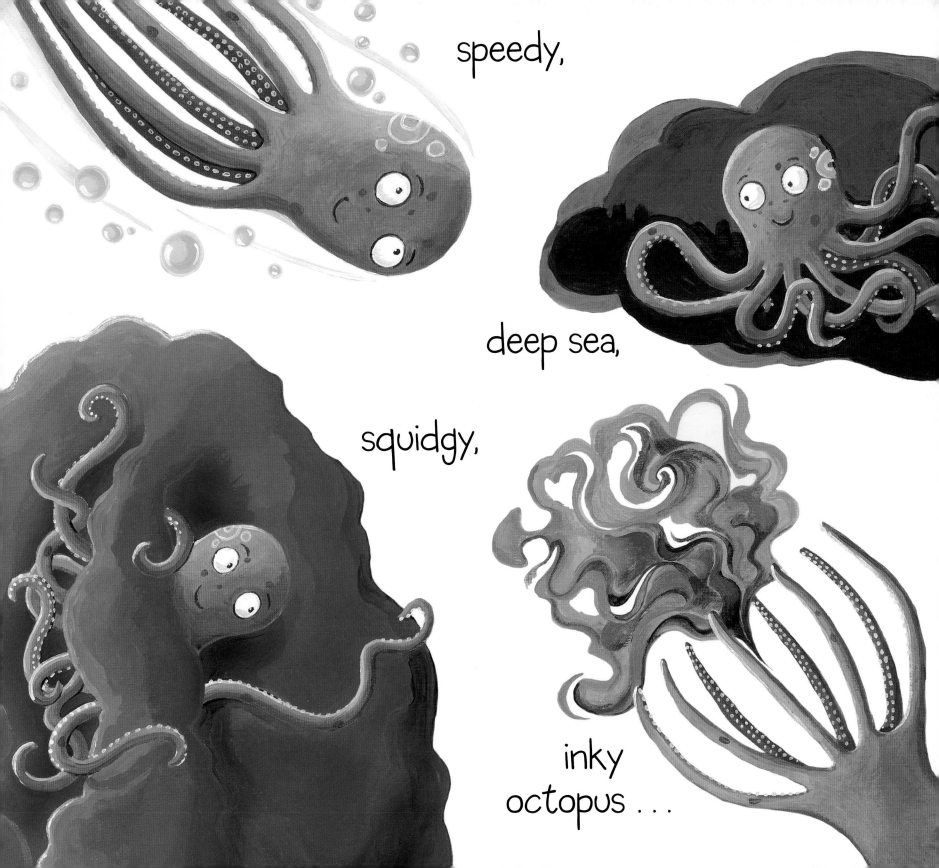

speedy,

deep sea,

squidgy,

inky
octopus . . .

"... but I'll still be a little bit tickly, too!"